Mr. Mean's Guide to
MANAGEMENT

Written by Adam Hargreaves and Andrew Langley
Illustrated by Adam Hargreaves

MR MEN AND LITTLE MISS™

& © 2000 Mrs Roger Hargreaves. Printed and published in 2000
under licence from Price Stern Sloan Inc., Los Angeles.

Published in Great Britain by Egmont World Limited,
a division of Egmont Holding Limited,
Deanway Technology Centre, Wilmslow Road, Handforth,
Cheshire SK9 3FB, UK.

Printed in Italy

ISBN 0 7498 4893 6

Mr. Mean's paper-clip rationing
didn't help office efficiency.

Mr. Small didn't enjoy
his stint in the post room.

Mr. Greedy checked his expenses.

The principle of telesales
was lost on Mr. Muddle.

After a frustrating morning at work,
Mr. Grumpy left early.

Mr. Tall just wasn't cut out for commuting.

Mr. Mean's budget for company vehicles disappointed the sales reps.

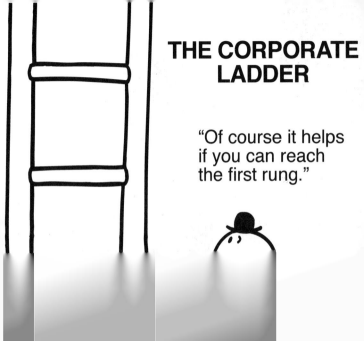

THE CORPORATE LADDER

"Of course it helps if you can reach the first rung."

Mr. Uppity

"What qualifications
do you have?"

"I'm extremely
good at twiddling
my thumbs."

Mr. Funny

'Petty' was not a word Mr. Mean ever associated with cash.

Mr. Funny spent a lot of time out on the fire escape after the office no-joking policy was implemented.

Mr. Dizzy always had great difficulty finding his desk each morning.

Mr. Silly hung the spreadsheets out to dry.

"Now I understand the meaning of 'work like a dog'....

      fetch this ...
      fetch that ...
      fetch this ...
      fetch that ..."

Little Miss Splendid

Mr. Uppity

Mr. Daydream

"JOIN THE GERBIL RACE."

Mr. Muddle

"It's all very well being a
big fish in a small pond;
but I'm still on dry land."

Mr. Small

"He's had his nose to the grindstone for too long."

Mr. Nosey

It wasn't that his job was boring, it was just that Mr. Funny was really enjoying his swivel chair.

Mr. Mean's annual bonus scheme
failed to create much of an incentive.

Mr. Mean's vending machine.

Little Miss Bossy had all the necessary qualities for her new role in the company.

Little Miss Chatterbox's meetings often overran.

Mr Quiet's position in the company
didn't bare much relation to his
original job description.

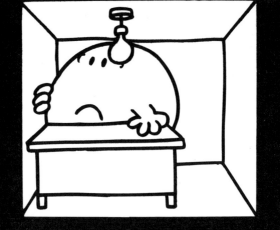

Mr. Happy's new office wasn't exactly how he had imagined it would be.

"I think I might retire after lunch."

Mr. Lazy

Mr. Uppity believed that
the size of your chair corresponded to
your status in the business world.

Lunch had not been the same since Mr. Mean had hired Mr. Skinny as Catering Manager.

Mr. Lazy takes the concept of home working to new levels.

A TIDY DESK MEANS A TIDY MIND.

It was proving awkward to retrieve documents from Mr. Silly's new filing system.

Post-it notes were the bane of Mr. Lazy's life

Mr. Greedy's Porkpie Chart

MR. BUMP'S BUSINESS TRIP

SALESMAN OF THE YEAR

AND LAST YEAR
AND THE YEAR
BEFORE LAST
AND THE ONE
PREVIOUS TO
THAT.
IN FACT EVERY
SINGLE YEAR
HE'S WORKED
HERE.

Mr. Perfect

One way to achieve early retirement.

Mr. Mischief

The photocopier
had never been the same
since Mr. Greedy's office party trick.

Mr. Happy regretted saying
Good Morning to Mr. Chatterbox.

Mr. Muddle found the filing very hard work.

"The gravy train, lolly, a mint, bread, fat cats, greed ... ummm, I don't think I have the appetite for big business.

Mr. Skinny